Meet Gabby and Gigi

...

Phnesha Marchette

ISBN 10: 1517458560
ISBN 13: 9781517458560
Library of Congress Control Number: 2015915599
CreateSpace Independent Publishing Platform
North Charleston, South Carolina

Dedicated to my mommy, Joann, who still tells me I can be anything I want to be!

Hi! My name is Gabby.
I am the big sister.

Because I love to kick!

We have two dogs. Our dogs are from the animal shelter. We like to hold them like babies.

This dog's name is Coffee.

This dog's name is Daisy.

We teach them tricks.

And they give us kisses.

We teach them manners, just like Mommy and Daddy teach us.

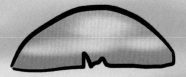

Time to get clean.

Time to rest your body.

We like to play ball on the beach.

We like to make castles on the beach.

And we have family movie night.

On Saturdays, we have play dates with our friends, Emma and Lizzy. We love to play in our room with our toys.

And we pretend we are rock stars.

We love to do many fun things!

Being together!

Let's see if you remember the story!

What kinds of things do Gabby and Gigi like to do?

What is the thing Gabby and Gigi love to do the most?

What are the names of Gabby and Gigi's dogs?

What do Gabby and Gigi teach their dogs?

Gabby and Gigi live near the mountains (true/false).

Gigi is the big sister (true/false).

Gabby likes ballet (true/false).

On a separate sheet of paper, draw something you like to do.

38694326R00023

Made in the USA
Middletown, DE
23 December 2016